ROBOTS

by Tammy Gagne

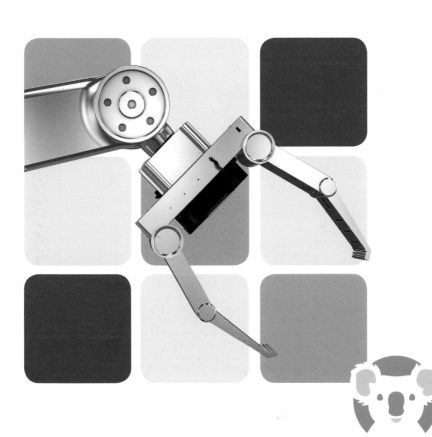

Cody Koala

An Imprint of Pop!
popbooksonline.com

abdopublishing.com
Published by Pop!, a division of ABDO, PO Box 398166, Minneapolis,
Minnesota 55439. Copyright © 2019 by POP, LLC. International copyrights
reserved in all countries. No part of this book may be reproduced in any
form without written permission from the publisher. Pop!™ is a trademark
and logo of POP, LLC.

Printed in the United States of America, North Mankato, Minnesota
042018
092018

THIS BOOK CONTAINS
RECYCLED MATERIALS
Distributed in paperback by North Star Editions, Inc.

Cover Photo: Shutterstock Images
Interior Photos: Shutterstock Images, 1, 5 (top), 5 (bottom left), 5 (bottom
right), 6, 9, 13, 14, 17 (left top), 17 (left middle), 17 (left bottom), 17 (right top),
17 (right middle top), 17 (right middle bottom); iStockphoto, 11; Michael
Kappeler/picture-alliance/dpa/AP Images, 17 (right bottom); Friso Gentsch/
picture-alliance/dpa/AP Images, 19; Hu Xuejun/Imaginechina/AP Images,
20

Editor: Charly Haley
Series Designer: Laura Mitchell

Library of Congress Control Number: 2017963465
Publisher's Cataloging-in-Publication Data
Names: Gagne, Tammy, author.
Title: Robots / by Tammy Gagne.
Description: Minneapolis, Minnesota : Pop!, 2019. | Series: 21st century
    inventions | Includes online resources and index.
Identifiers: ISBN 9781532160424 (lib.bdg.) | ISBN 9781635177930 (pbk) | ISBN
    9781532161544 (ebook) |
Subjects: LCSH: Robots--Juvenile literature. | Robot industry--Juvenile
    literature. | Technological innovations--Juvenile literature. | Inventions-
    -History--Juvenile literature. | Technology--History--Juvenile literature.
Classification: DDC 609--dc23

Cody Koala

Pop open this book and you'll find QR codes like this one, loaded with information, so you can learn even more!

Scan this code* and others like it while you read, or visit the website below to make this book pop.

popbooksonline.com/robots

*Scanning QR codes requires a web-enabled smart device with a QR code reader app and a camera.

Table of Contents

Chapter 1

What Are Robots?

Robots are machines that perform tasks for people. Some robots are simple. Robot vacuums are one example. Other robots are very complex.

Watch a video here!

Some robots put together cars. Some robots build things in factories. Other robots explore space.

Some robots can help doctors perform **surgery**.

Chapter 2

How Robots Work

It may look like robots think for themselves. But people tell robots what to do. People use computer **programming** to do this.

Learn more here!

In computer programming, a person writes a list of commands. Each robot has a computer inside. This computer follows the commands. It tells the robots parts to move.

Chapter 3

Ways to Use Robots

People can use robots to do **chores**. Some robots can clean a cat's litter box. Others can mow the lawn or clean rain gutters.

Some toy robots act like pet dogs. They play fetch and learn tricks.

Learn more here!

The military uses robots for many things. Some of those robots can fly high in the sky. They can take pictures from above.

Robots help some kids go to school while they stay at home. Students can move the robot from one class to another. They can see through its camera. They can even talk with their teachers and friends.

Types of Robots

Simple - - - - - -> **Complex**

robot vacuum

factory robot

robot toy dog

military robot

space robot

robot lawn mower

robot that goes to school

Chapter 4

The Future of Robots

The **technology** around robots is still developing. People are working to make robots better and better.

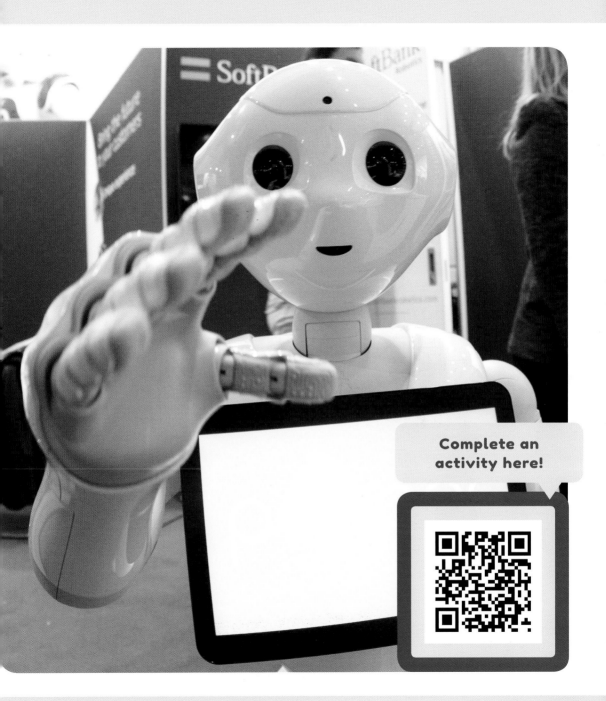

Complete an activity here!

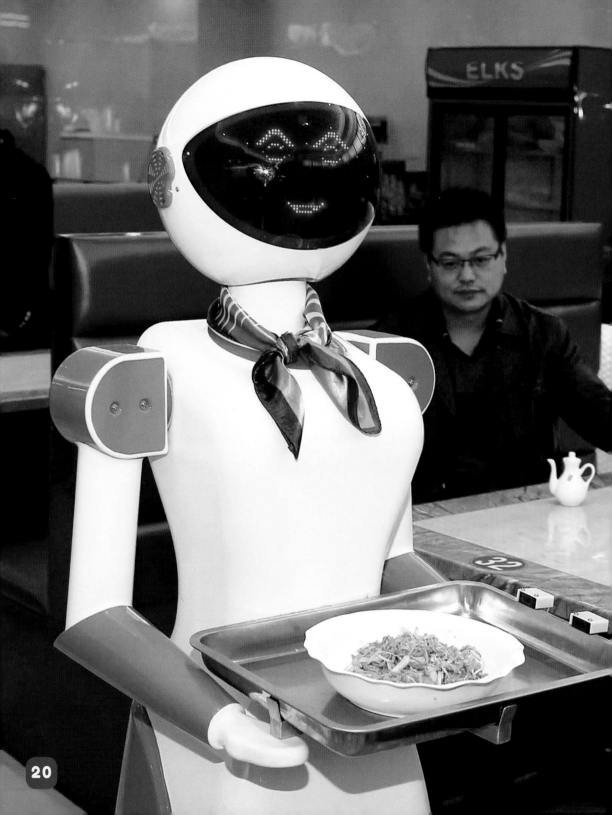

In the future, robots may do more jobs for people. Robots may work at restaurants. They may help take care of elderly people.

Making Connections

Text-to-Self

Have you ever used a robot? Or have you seen someone else use a robot?

Text-to-Text

Have you read another book about robots or other modern technology? What did you learn from this book?

Text-to-World

How do you think robots can change the world?

Glossary

chore – a common household task.

programming – instructions for a computer.

surgery – a medical operation.

technology – objects created by using science.

Index

Online Resources

popbooksonline.com

Thanks for reading this Cody Koala book!

Scan this code* and others like it in this book, or visit the website below to make this book pop!

popbooksonline.com/robots

*Scanning QR codes requires a web-enabled smart device with a QR code reader app and a camera.